# Books by Jil Ross

## DATE DUE

*This book is dedicated to my aunts:*

Dorothy *"Auntie"* Davis

Burma Weekley

Marguerite McCrary

Mattie Broome

Velma *"Honey"* Bragg

Gloria Simpson

Tahira Lateef

Gus Marie Pyles

Marie Hutton

Ruth Bowens

&

Ella Curtis

*You've all been such great inspirations to me. Through your words and/or actions, you've all taught me valuable life lessons.*

# Words to Look For & Their Meanings:

CONCENTRATE

Pronounced: kon-sin-trat
(verb) - to focus intently

INDIGNANT

Pronounced: in-dig-nent
(adjective) a feeling of anger

DETENTION

Pronounced: de-ten-shin
(noun) to be detained, a punishment

CRESTFALLEN

Pronounced: krest-fah-lun
(adjective) – disappointed, dejected, depressed

LEVITATE

Pronounced: lev-i-tayt
(verb) to rise in the air or float

# Chapter 1

Another weekend had passed. It was Monday morning and Foster was sitting in homeroom. As soon as the 8:45 A.M. bell rang, Mrs. Princeton took attendance. Once she finished taking attendance she began making announcements of the different events going on at school that week.

"Those students planning on competing in the spelling-bee should meet with Ms. Paige in the library during recess today," she said. Foster sat there staring out of the window; he was completely uninterested in what Mrs. Princeton was saying. "Oh, this is interesting," Mrs. Princeton said enthusiastically, "The science club will meet after school to compare different insect species." Foster chuckled as he watched the girls in his class squirm when the teacher said the word 'insect'.

Mrs. Princeton continued, "Tomorrow the glee club will meet in the auditorium to practice for Friday's assembly."

*"Bo-r-r-ring,"* Foster mumbled under his breath.

Mrs. Princeton cleared her throat, peered over the top of her glasses, looked at Foster and asked, "Foster, is there something you'd like to say? I think I heard you mumble something."

"Ah, no, ma'am," he said looking down at the floor and embarrassed that she had heard him. He could hear some of his classmates snickering.

"And for those of you who are interested, there will be auditions held this Thursday after school for this year's school play, 'The Life and Times of King Tutankhamen', also known as King Tut." Mrs. Princeton continued, "There will be a notice posted on the auditorium door by the end of school today telling what the various characters' parts will be, as well as what you'll need to have prepared for the audition."

"YES!" exclaimed Foster loudly. This caused his classmates to turn and stare at him.

"Foster Blake, please contain yourself, you're not on the playground, you know," Mrs. Princeton frowned. Foster had a hard time concentrating on his school lessons from that moment on.

Last year he wanted to be in the school play 'Humpty Dumpty Was Pushed', but he'd gotten the chicken pox and missed the audition. He promised himself that this year he'd win himself a part in the play, no matter what.

# Chapter 2

As soon as the 2:30 P.M. bell rang Foster dashed from the classroom and ran down the hall towards the auditorium to see what parts were going to be available for the play.

*"Oh boy, competition is going to be tough,"* he thought to himself. From a distance he could see that a crowd was forming around the auditorium door where the play auditions were posted.

Some of the students who were in the back of the crowd were standing on their books trying to read the posting, other students were trying to jump above the crowd to see. It was at times like these that Foster was glad he was taller than the average boy his age.

He walked up behind the crowd and read the poster.

LOOKING FOR STUDENTS TO AUDITION FOR THE PLAY: 'THE LIFE AND TIMES OF KING TUT'. PLEASE COME PREPARED THURSDAY AT 2:45 P.M. TO RECITE A POEM OR DRAMATIC READING NO MORE THAN ONE MINUTE IN LENGTH.

"I thought I'd find you here," his sister Marie said. "I was standing in the playground waiting for you and then I remembered about the auditions. So, are you going to tryout?" she asked.

"Yes, I am. And not only am I going to tryout, but I am going to get my self a part in the play," Foster answered. He was very sure of himself. "What about you? Are you going to tryout?" Foster asked his sister.

"No, I talked to Mr. Rossi and Ms. Blair, they said that I could work on the set design and on the costumes which is way more exciting to me than having to memorize lines and learn stage directions."

"Cool," Foster said. "Like Grandma Judy always says, 'different strokes for different folks.'"

Foster and Marie left school and walked home.

# Chapter 3

Once the children were home, Marie asked her brother, "Foster, do you want to play a game of chess after we finish our homework?"

"Nope," Foster replied.

"How about a game of checkers? I'll even let you win," Marie said sarcastically.

"Not interested," he said.

Marie looked at him curiously; she put her finger on her chin, and then said "Okay, you win. I'll challenge you to a game of Wizard Gizzard on the computer and I'll give you a ten point lead, how about it?"

"Negative. I have an important project to work on." He walked away and offered no other explanation, which made Marie even more curious.

The children sat at the table in the family room and did their homework quietly while their mother prepared dinner. On most evenings Foster would just sit at the table daydreaming or he would tease Marie and would have to be reminded by their mother several times to finish his homework.

But on this particular evening Foster completed his homework in record time. Work that usually took Foster one to two hours to complete only took 45 minutes.

As soon as Foster finished his homework he put his books away and headed to the recreation room.

The children's mother was in the kitchen stirring a pot of delicious smelling red beans and rice when she heard something that surprised her.

She stopped stirring and listened. She followed the sound to the next room. "Foster," she asked, "Honey, what are you doing?"

Foster looked up at his mother and said "I'm practicing my drum lesson."

"I can see that. What I mean is that I usually have to ask you (*and sometimes even beg you, she thought*) a couple of times to sit down and practice."

Foster smiled at his mother, shrugged his shoulders and said, "Just doing what I have to do, Mom."

She stared at him for a moment and then went back to the kitchen and finished preparing dinner.

Marie had completed her homework and was in the kitchen sampling a spoonful of red beans and rice when Foster walked in with his jacket on. He was heading for the door.

Marie jumped up from the table practically spitting out the food in her mouth and shouted, "I knew it! He just wants to go over to Phillip's house and play video games, but he knows the rule, no visiting friends on school nights."

Foster completely ignored Marie and said to his mother, "I'm going to walk DJ now, if that's alright."

"Well, sure." she said with a surprised look on her face.

"What's the matter Mom, are you O.K?" he asked.

"I'm fine," she said. Now she had a curious look on her face, too.

As soon as Foster was out the door Marie and her mother gave each other that *'What's Foster up to'* look. Then Marie said, "Something's going on with that brother of mine and I'm going find out what."

# Chapter 4

By the time Foster returned from walking the dog, his father was home from work. The family sat down at the dining room table and ate their dinner. Foster quickly finished his dinner, and asked if he could be excused. He cleaned his eating space and proceeded upstairs to his bedroom and closed the door.

As soon as Foster was out of sight, Marie winked at her parents and said, "Don't worry. I'm going to get to the bottom of this."

Marie tiptoed up the stairs quietly. Foster thought he heard a noise in the hallway and opened his bedroom door to check who or what was there.

He didn't see anything because Marie was hiding behind the tall Ficus tree in the hallway.

Once Foster went back into his room and shut the door Marie put her ear to the door. She could hear Foster saying something but she could not figure out what. Before Marie had a chance to hide behind the Ficus tree again, Foster had pulled the door open and Marie fell right on the floor.

"And just what do you think you're doing?" Foster asked.

Marie acted indignant and demanded, "Me? What about you? What are you doing? Why are you acting so strange?"

Foster shook his head and explained, "I am not acting strange. I'm preparing for Thursday's audition. I wanted to get my school work, drum practice and chores out of the way so that I could get in as much rehearsal time as I could before I go to bed."

"Oh, I see. Well, what are you going to recite?" Marie asked

"I'm going to recite a poem from my book, *Mr. Marble*," he told her.

"You don't need to practice any of those poems. You know all of them," Marie said.

"You can never be too prepared," Foster said as he picked up his book and continued to recite the poem he'd selected.

As Marie began walking out of Foster's room she turned and warned him "Foster, do you remember that movie we watched when the guy kept practicing a song over and over again, and then when it was time for him to sing the song he'd forgotten all the words? Well, if that happens to you remind me *not* to say 'I told you so.'"

# Chapter 5

Thursday had rolled around before Foster knew it. The day had started off as usual with Mrs. Princeton's boring announcements. Foster had such anticipation about the play auditions that once again he found it hard to concentrate on his schoolwork.

Mrs. Princeton called on Foster to answer the question, "What is the name of the current president?" He leaped from his desk and exclaimed, "Mr. Marble!" His classmates laughed hysterically, but his teacher did not think his outburst was funny.

Since she had to spend the next fifteen minutes getting the class settled, she announced to Foster, in front of his classmates, "You'll spend thirty minutes after school serving a detention which will consist of you cleaning the chalkboards."

Foster was now in a panic, he jumped up and blurted out, "Oh no, Mrs. Princeton, I can't serve a detention today because I have to…"

But before he could finish his sentence Mrs. Princeton cut his words off and said, "Excuse me Foster, I was not asking you if you would mind serving a detention, *I was telling you that you **will** serve one.* You see Foster, It's *not* an option. Do *you* understand *me*?"

Foster was crestfallen. "Yes, ma'am," he said as he took his seat.

As soon as the 2:30 P.M. dismissal bell rang he ran right from the gym to his homeroom and began cleaning the chalk boards. Before getting a detention, Foster had planned on finding a quiet place in the library after school so that he could practice his lines, his pitch and his enunciation before going to the audition, but now he had to practice while cleaning the chalkboards.

Foster had served 25 of the 30 minutes of his detention when Mrs. Princeton, who was trying to grade book reports said, "Goodness gracious, Foster, what in the world are you over there mumbling?"

He explained to her that he was repeating his lines from his favorite poem before the audition. She found his reciting to be so annoying that she excused him from his detention early, practically begging him to hurry-up and leave.

Marie was unaware that her brother had a detention, and had gone to the auditorium immediately after school to support him.

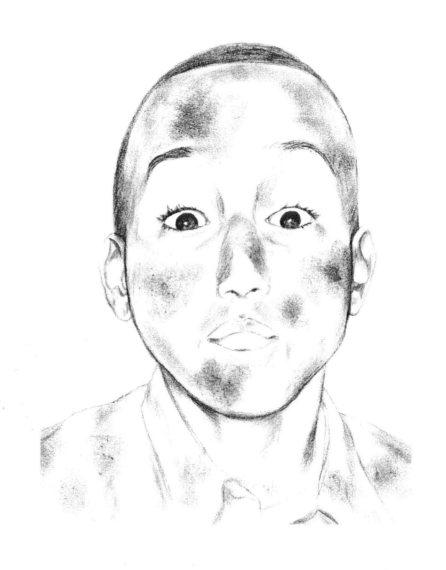

# Chapter 6

Foster ran from the classroom to his locker. He grabbed his jacket and his uneaten lunch, he had spent his entire lunch and recess going over the lines of the poem. He ran down the hall so fast that he did not notice that the school custodian, Mr. Dane, was mopping the floor.

Before Mr. Dane could get the words out of his mouth and warn Foster to "slow down," Foster was sliding down the hall.

"Whoa!" Foster exclaimed. He was trying to balance himself as if he were on a skateboard. Finally he landed on his bottom, right in front of the auditorium door. With all of the running and sliding, Foster had not realized that his face, hands and clothes were covered with chalk and water. He looked pale and gooey.

Just as he was running through the door to the auditorium he heard Mr. Rossi saying, "If there are no other students who want to recite this will conclude the…"

"Me, me you didn't audition me!" Foster interrupted. All heads turned.

"Where have you been, and what's all that stuff on your face and clothes?" Marie demanded.

He ran right pass Marie and paid no attention to what she was asking him. In fact, he was running so fast that he tripped and rolled toward the stage.

"Slow down young man!" Mr. Rossi scolded. "Now, have you prepared a poem?" he asked.

"Yes, sir" Foster said.

"Well, go on. Get on the stage and let's hear what you've got to say," Mr. Rossi said impatiently, as he pointed toward the stage.

Foster was still out of breath. He followed Mr. Rossi's instructions and went up on the stage to stand directly under the hot spotlight. He opened his mouth to speak, but nothing came out.

"Please, go ahead young man" Mr. Rossi said. Foster continued to stand there with his mouth open and still nothing came out.

Marie could hear some of the students laughing at Foster. She turned and gave them a mean look. Then she turned back around and put her hands on her face and said to herself, "Oh no, I *knew* this was going to happen."

Mr. Rossi was losing his patience. "Young man, do you or don't you have a poem prepared?" he asked in a stern voice. Foster just stood there, staring into the bright light looking pale, wet and gooey. He said nothing. "That's enough, Foster, you may come down off the stage now," said Mr. Rossi.

He then turned to the audience and announced that this would conclude the auditions. He reminded the boys and girls that the assigned parts would be posted on the auditorium door tomorrow morning before school.

Marie felt sad for her brother. She knew how much he'd practiced that poem and how badly he wanted to be in the play. Marie picked up Fosters book bag and lunch bag and carried them home for him.

Foster was disappointed with himself. He was so nervous when he got up on stage to recite the poem that he could not speak. While walking home Foster confided in his sister, "Marie, I don't know what happened. I looked out at the audience and saw my classmates and the teachers; at first my stomach got butterflies and then my hands started to sweat, and then my mouth got dry, and then I had brain freeze."

"Foster, you had a bad case of nerves, that's all. Don't worry, there's always next year."

Foster and Marie walked the rest of the way home in silence.

# Chapter 7

On Friday when Foster walked into school he could see a group of students around the auditorium door. He did not want to be reminded of his disastrous audition the day before and walked briskly past the crowd.

Foster's friend Jordan was standing around the door when he noticed Foster and shouted out "Hey Foster, you..." But Foster pretended not to hear him and continued walking towards the classroom. Foster thought to himself, *"If Jordan's my friend, why is he reminding me of how awful I did yesterday?"*

As soon as Foster got settled in his seat the bell rang and Mrs. Princeton took attendance and started with the announcements. Foster put his head down on the desk and covered it with a notebook. "My first announcement is to congratulate a student in this homeroom who was awarded a part in this year's play."

Foster mumbled under his breath, *"This woman obviously gets pleasure in torturing me."* He dismissed his thought when he heard Mrs. Princeton say, "Class, let's give Foster a round of applause on being awarded a part in the play."

When Foster heard this he sat straight up in his seat and said, "What? What did you say? Will you please repeat that?" Foster could not believe what he was hearing.

Mrs. Princeton cleared her throat and said, "Foster, play or no play you are still required to raise your hand when you want to speak in this class, do you understand?"

"Yes, ma'am" Foster said. He was so anxious that once again he was unable to concentrate on his school lessons.

At lunch time Foster ran directly to the auditorium to read the posting. Foster was elated to find that he had been awarded the part of the *mummy*. He had no lines to memorize, he had nothing to say, and at the end of the play he would get to be levitated above the audience on a cable cord.

All Foster had to do for the most part was lay flat and be wrapped in gauze bandage.

"Cool!" Foster exclaimed. After school Marie and Jordan ran up to Foster to congratulate him. Jordan gave Foster a high five and said, "You got the best part in the play."

Marie sarcastically said, "I suppose, if you consider playing a **dummy** the best part."

Jordan corrected Marie, "Not a **dummy** Marie, a *mummy*."

Marie rolled her eyes and said "*Mummy*, **dummy**, what's the difference?"

Jordan explained, "Marie there's a big difference. A *mummy* is a dead body that has been preserved in oils and salts then wrapped in cloth. This is an ancient process that was used to make a body last a long time after death. The body was then put inside of a really fancy coffin, called a 'sarcophagus'. I know this because I got an 'A' on my history test that covered the era of ancient Egypt."

Marie rolled her eyes at Jordan.

"Yeah, Marie," Foster continued, "And a **dummy**, on the other hand, is either an imitation person, like what we saw in that commercial in those car crash tests, or a **dummy** is a stupid person. And I am neither of those."

"Well…," Marie said, needing to have the last word, "My friend Kourtney said that you're a **dummy,**" as she nudged her brother in the arm.

"Well, Kourtney doesn't know what she's talking about." Foster replied.

Jordan said goodbye to Foster and Marie and went to catch the school bus. Foster pleaded with his sister, "Marie, I know that it's very hard for you to keep a secret, but I would like for you to *please* not tell anyone about my part in the play. I want to surprise everyone the night of the play. You can tell them I'm in the play…just not *what* I am in the play."

Marie answered, "Sure, Foster, you know your secret is safe with me."

# Chapter 8

As soon as Foster got home from school he went to the den where his mother was working on the computer and told her the good news that he had gotten a part in the play, but not which part he was playing.

"I can't wait to see you in the play, I know that you'll do a fine job," his mother said.

When Foster went upstairs to put his school things away, Marie entered the room. "Did Foster tell you that he's in the school play?" Marie asked.

"Yes," their mother replied with a big smile on her face.

Marie then asked, "Well, did he tell you that he is playing a **dummy** in the play? -Oops! I think I wasn't supposed to tell you that. He wanted to surprise you."

"Marie, did I hear you just say that Foster is a **dummy** in the play?" their mother asked with a concerned look on her face.

"Yes, ma'am," said Marie, not realizing that she'd made a mistake. Then she grabbed her jump rope and went outside to play.

"*My* Foster playing a **dummy**, well, I'll see about that." Mrs. Blake paused from her work and thought about the time when Foster fixed her computer just in time to complete an important presentation for work. The thought of Foster playing a **dummy** was quite upsetting to her. "*Maybe if I go and talk to Mr. Rossi and tell him how smart Foster is, he will re-cast him in a different part*," their mother thought to herself.

Marie played with her jump rope on the driveway, while her father watered the lawn. Marie's father asked her, "Did anything special happen at school today?"

"No, not really," Marie answered. Then she continued, "Oh yeah, Foster is going to be a **dummy** in the school play."

The children's father, who was shocked, responded, "He's going to play a what?"

"A **dummy**," Marie said, again not realizing that what she was saying was wrong and forgetting that she'd made Foster a promise.

Mr. Blake had become so distracted by this news that he allowed the water hose to slip from his hands and water was shooting all over the yard now, as well as on himself and Marie.

Their father also found this announcement quite disturbing. As far as he was concerned his son was too smart to be a **dummy**, even if it was just playing one in the school play. He got control of the water hose and continued to water the grass. As he tended to the lawn he reflected on the time, while out on a camping trip, Foster lead his scout troop to safety when they got lost in the forest during a storm.

Marie told her father that she was going in the house to see if dinner was almost done. Mr. Blake didn't even hear her speak, he was talking to himself "*I think if I go up to the school, I can talk to Mr. Rossi, 'man to man', and explain to him that he made a bad choice in casting Foster as a* **dummy.**"

As Marie walked in the door the phone rang. "Marie I'm putting dinner rolls in the oven, will you please answer the phone? And if it's your grandmother, let her know that dinner will be ready in twenty minutes, please," her mother said.

Marie answered the phone. "Hi, Grandma Judy... Yes, dinner is almost ready... Guess what?" she continued, "Foster is going to be the **dummy** in the school play."

"What!" Grandma was so loud that Marie had to take the phone away from her ear! Clearly, the children's grandmother was infuriated when she heard this news.

As soon as she got off the phone with Marie, she grabbed her sweater, hat and keys, and headed out the door. As she was on her way she began to talk to herself out loud, not caring who heard her, *"Those people at that school must be nuts if they want my little sweetie to play like he's a dummy. Clearly that director is unaware that Foster was smart enough to navigate how to get my over-sized*

41

*recliner thru the door when the movers could not even figure it out!"*

She had also decided to pay a visit to the school before the play and have a talk with the director to get to the bottom of this madness.

# Chapter 9

By the time Grandma got to the house, dinner was ready and the table was set. The children's mother, father and grandmother were all so angry, since Marie told them that Foster would play a **dummy** in the play, that none of them had much of an appetite.

In fact, they hardly even talked during dinner. The three of them mostly sat there with *phony* teeth-gritting smiles on their faces as they watched Foster eat.

Finally, the children's mother asked, "Foster, when is the play?"

Enthusiastically, Foster answered, "In two weeks! I can hardly wait!"

"*Poor thing*," his mother thought, "*He has no idea that a **dummy** is not an honorable part to play.*"

His father thought to himself "*What a trooper. He's playing a **dummy** and he's so proud. I guess he's going to be 'the best little **dummy** he can be'.*"

As the children's grandmother was sitting there taking all of this in, her eyes filled with tears. Foster's grandmother, who was overly emotional, looked at him and said, "Kid, you have a lot of spunk and character, even if you are a **dummy**."

Then she excused herself from the table, shaking her head as she walked out of the room. Foster had no idea what his grandmother was talking about. As a matter of fact, he thought that

46

his mother, father and grandmother were acting kind of weird, and he had no idea why. He sat there and enjoyed his dinner.

The adults had each decided not to speak with Mr. Rossi. After witnessing how comfortable Foster was with the part he was playing, they thought it would be best if they did not interfere. They would just 'support the **dummy.**'

# Chapter 10

Two weeks had passed and the night of the play had finally arrived. Foster's family had gotten to the theater early to ensure that they would get seats close to the stage.

The lights went down, the curtain came up and it was time for the play to begin. At the end of the play, the mummy of King Tut was presented. The tomb opened up and there was Foster wrapped in white cloth and bandage.

He was levitated from the tomb with the help of the stage crew pulling a cable cord. The audience looked up and "Oohhh-ed" and "Ahhh-ed!" He had performed his part perfectly and did not make a single mistake. Everyone in the audience clapped.

Foster's family was very proud of him. They stood outside the stage door waiting for him to come out. They were going to Foster's favorite restaurant to celebrate his exceptional performance.

Foster's mother, father and grandmother all turned to Marie and said in unison, "Foster played a MUMMY not a **dummy!**"

Marie just looked down at the ground, put her hands over her mouth, shrugged her shoulders and said, "Oops."

Foster overheard this exchange and said to his sister, "Marie, I asked you not to tell anyone that I was playing a mummy in the play, and you promised not to tell."

Marie attempted to squirm her way out of the situation by explaining, "Well, Foster, I guess I didn't *really* tell your secret since I told them you were a **dummy,** not a mummy."

Marie's father looked her directly in the eye and said, "Marie, you're missing the point. You told a secret AND you spread wrong information. As a result, you got your mother, grandmother and me all worked up and in a frenzy. You were wrong and you should realize that."

Marie thought about what her father had said. She felt bad. "Foster," she said in a sincere voice, "I'm sorry. I did not tell your secret on purpose. I was just so happy that you got a part in the play that I wanted to spread the news to everyone."

Foster smiled, "Okay, Marie, you're forgiven."

Marie then turned to her parents and grandmother and apologized for passing incorrect information, and then added, "Boy, do I feel like a big **dummy**!"

Everyone laughed!

# THE END

# QUESTIONS FOR THOUGHT & DISCUSSION

1. Have you ever had to audition? If, so, what did you audition for? Were you nervous?

2. Foster got a detention for disrupting the class. Have you ever gotten a detention? If so, what could you have done differently to avoid the detention?

3. Why do you think Marie carried Foster's book bag and lunch home for him?

4. Have you ever felt disappointed before? If so, why?

5. Have you ever felt embarrassed before? If so, why?

6. What was wrong with what Marie had done?

7. Have you ever felt proud of yourself? Explain.

8. Do you think Foster and Marie's parents overreacted to Marie's misinformation?

# *About the Author*

*Photo by Shakir Karriem*

Jil Ross began writing 12 years ago, while recuperating from a broken leg. As her children got older, she wrote about the various antics and mischief they got themselves into. Her children are the inspiration for many of her writings. She lives with her husband and two children in Chicago, Illinois.